Disney

PIRATES
of the
CARIBBEAN
DEAD MAN'S CHEST

Illustrated by Art Mawhinney

Copyright © 2006 Disney Enterprises, Inc.

Based on the screenplay written by Ted Elliott & Terry Rossio
Based on characters created by Ted Elliott & Terry Rossio and
Stuart Beattie and Jay Wolpert
Based on Walt Disney's Pirates of the Caribbean
Produced by Jerry Bruckheimer
Directed by Gore Verbinski

Published by Louis Weber, C.E.O., Publications International, Ltd.
7373 North Cicero Avenue, Lincolnwood, Illinois 60712

Ground Floor, 59 Gloucester Place, London W1U 8JJ

Customer Service: 1-800-595-8484 or
customer_service@pilbooks.com

www.pilbooks.com

Look and Find is a registered trademark of
Publications International, Ltd.

b i kids is a registered trademark of
Publications International, Ltd.

8 7 6 5 4 3 2 1
ISBN-13: 978-1-4127-6377-6
ISBN-10: 1-4127-6377-0

 publications international, ltd.

A visit from Lord Beckett has ruined Elizabeth and Will's wedding! They have been arrested for helping Captain Jack Sparrow. As redcoats swarm the scene, see if you can find these marines.

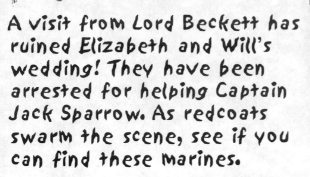

Shorty

Speedy

Slim

Freckles

Red

Wink

Oh no—Captain Jack Sparrow has been marked with the Black Spot! This means Davy Jones has sent the Kraken after him. While Jack figures out what to do, look around the *Black Pearl* for these precious gems.

Green emerald

Purple amethyst

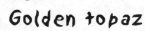

Golden topaz

Blue sapphire

White diamond

Red ruby

Beckett offers to drop the charges against Elizabeth and Will...but only if Will can retrieve Captain Jack Sparrow's Compass. Look around the office of the East India Trading Company to find these other navigational tools.

Globe

Astrolabe

Logline

Wind rose

Spyglass

Divider

Sextant

Captain Jack Sparrow has somehow become Chief of the Tribe of Pelegostos. This is not a tribe you want to invite home for dinner, if you know what we mean. Look around the island to find some vegetarian dining options.

Watermelon

Passion fruit

Breadfruit

Jackfruit

Avocado

Star fruit

Bunch of bananas

Pineapple

Jack and Will seek help from Tia Dalma. She will know where to find the key to Davy Jones's chest. Look around her home to find these bewitched keys.

Key to success

Key to failure

Key to despair

Key to happiness

Key to understanding

Key to confusion

If you dare, search the tortured crew of the *Flying Dutchman* to find these poor souls who slave for Davy Jones.

Koleniko

Bootstrap Bill

Jimmy Legs

Maccus

Greenbeard

Penrod

Crash

Tortuga is the last place you'll find an honest man, but it's the first place to look for pirates. While Captain Jack looks for 99 souls to give to Davy Jones, see if you can find these other pirates lurking in the cantina.

Jolly Roger

Shoreditch

Lefteye de Theo

Barberossa

Gilbert N. Sullivan III

William Kid

Peg

Davy Jones's chest is buried on *Isla Cruces*—and everyone wants it! Who will get the chest? What does it contain? Ponder these questions as you look for these other sought-after items.

Letters of Marque

Jar of dirt

The key

Captain Jack's Compass

The small chest

The large chest

Cask

Find the remnants of Elizabeth's big day.

- [ ] Something old
- [ ] Something new
- [ ] Something borrowed
- [ ] Something blue
- [ ] Bouquet
- [ ] Wedding gift
- [ ] Wedding rings
- [ ] Wedding cake

There are other black spots on the Black Pearl. Can you find them?

- [ ] Dice
- [ ] Head rag
- [ ] A mounted fish
- [ ] A pair of bloomers
- [ ] A polka-dotted pennant
- [ ] Sheet music

Look around Beckett's office for souvenirs from his trading and travels around the world.

- [ ] Mask
- [ ] Boomerang
- [ ] Wooden shoe
- [ ] Dancing Shiva
- [ ] Jade dragon
- [ ] Totem
- [ ] Aztec calendar

The Black Pearl's resident ghost monkey fits right in with the Pelegostos. Can you find him, plus 5 more spider monkeys on the island?

Tia Dalma gives Jack a jar of dirt — a bit of land to keep him safe from the Kraken. Find these other jars in Tia's shack.

- ☐ Jar of bat wings
- ☐ Jar of beetles
- ☐ Jar of jellyfish
- ☐ Jar of crocodile teeth
- ☐ Jar of eyeballs
- ☐ Jar of snake rattles

Return to the Flying Dutchman to find these sea creature stowaways.

- ☐ Lobster
- ☐ Jellyfish
- ☐ Shark
- ☐ Manta ray
- ☐ Sea star
- ☐ Crab
- ☐ Eel

On Tortuga, when gold talks, people listen. Look for this loot that some scoundrels are flashing.

- ☐ Gold goblet
- ☐ Gold sword
- ☐ Gold brick
- ☐ Gold shell
- ☐ Gold watch
- ☐ Gold crown

With everyone prepared to do battle over Davy Jones's chest, there were a lot of swords drawn. In fact, there were 17 swords drawn. See if you can find them all.